2/18

Dial Books for Young Readers

HAMSTER PRINCESS
WHISKERELLA

HAMSTER PRINCESS
WHISKERELLA

BY
Ursula
Vernon

DIAL BOOKS FOR YOUNG READERS
PENGUIN YOUNG READERS GROUP
An imprint of Penguin Random House LLC
375 Hudson Street
New York, NY 10014

Printed in China
ISBN 9780399186554

10   9   8   7   6   5   4   3   2   1

Design by Jennifer Kelly
Text set in Minister Std Light

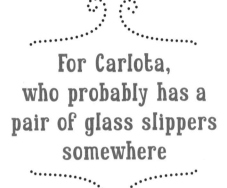

For Carlota,
who probably has a
pair of glass slippers
somewhere

HAMSTER PRINCESS

WHISKERELLA

CHAPTER 1

The castle of the hamster king was a bustle of activity. Servants ran back and forth, carrying tablecloths and platters of food, hanging banners from the battlements, and scouring the countryside for extra tables.

"Harriet!"

Through this controlled chaos, the voice of the hamster queen cut like an ax through warm butter.

"HARRIET!"

"I'm up here, Mom!" yelled Harriet Hamsterbone, princess of the hamster kingdom, slayer of Ogrecats, bane of giants, breaker of curses, and recreational cliff-diver.

"Are you ready?" called her mother, climbing the stairs to Harriet's bedroom. There were only ten stairs, since Harriet had moved out of the tower bedroom following the incident with the thorn hedges. "The guests will be here soon! You'll need to get . . ."

The hamster queen put her hand over her eyes. "Yes, but meeting the ambassador is only an excuse for the ball, dear."

"It is?" asked Harriet, still dangling from a curtain rod by her ankles.

"Yes. We've invited all the princes, you see."

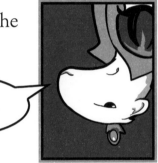

OH. THEM.

"They don't like me, Mom." (The feeling was mutual, but Harriet didn't want to get into that with her mother.)

"They're just intimidated by you, dear," said the hamster queen.

"And rightly so!" said Harriet, unhooking her ankles and falling in a heap on the floor. "I'm very intimidating! If you intimidate monsters, sometimes you don't even need to fight them. They just apologize and go away."

"Yes, dear," said the hamster queen. "But we're hoping that one of these princes will marry you."

I DON'T WANT TO GET MARRIED! I'M *TWELVE!*

IT'S NEVER TOO EARLY TO PLAN FOR YOUR FUTURE, DEAR. AFTER ALL, YOU DON'T WANT TO BE SLAYING MONSTERS WHEN YOU'RE OLD AND GRAY, DO YOU?

Her mother sighed heavily. "Well then, you'll need someone to look after the castle while you're away."

Harriet was forced to acknowledge the logic of this. She climbed to her feet. "Okay, maybe. But not one of these princes. They call me Crazy Princess Harriet. None of them are going to talk to me."

"That's the beauty of it," said her mother. "They won't know who you are. It's a costume ball!"

Harriet clasped her hands together, delighted. "Ooh! Really?"

Visions of costumes whirled through her mind. She could be a vampire—a witch—a ferocious Battle Hamster of the North, who wears a helmet with twisting horns and speaks in verse—

"Yes," said her mother. "The bat ambassador is very fond of costume balls, and everything came together beautifully. So everyone will be masked, and then—"

... YOU'RE WEARING A FANCY DRESS AND A MASK.

"Awwwwwwww," said Harriet. "*Moooooom!*"

"Don't *Moooooom* me, young lady! This is your chance to meet some nice young princes without terrifying them!"

Harriet groaned, her visions of Genghis Prawn slipping away. "But you always told me to be myself!"

"Yes," said her mother. "You *should* be yourself. It's just that when *you* are being yourself, it can be very alarming for innocent bystanders, and the stories tend to grow a bit when they're repeated. So this way, we'll all be masked and the princes can get to know you without your—ah—reputation preceding you. And if you hit it off with some nice young prince, by the time of the unmasking, the stories won't matter at all!"

Harriet felt that on some level this was completely wrong. But she also knew that there was no point in arguing when her mother had this look in her eye.

PUT THIS ON.

CHAPTER 2

The ball was going well by Harriet's mother's standards, which meant that Harriet was about to die of boredom.

She had talked to the bat ambassador at great length. He was a good-natured, inverted fellow very interested in opening up trade with the hamster kingdom. Her mother wouldn't let her hang upside down to talk to him, but he didn't seem to mind.

"Alas," said the bat ambassador. "I fear that sonar is a difficult skill to learn." He sipped his drink neatly, holding the glass right way up, and took a bite of a bug canapé. "And would you truly wish to sit and practice clicking at a very high pitch, when you could be dancing with princes?"

"Absolutely," said Harriet. "One hundred percent. No question." The ambassador laughed.

There were, in fact, three princes at the ball whom Harriet knew already. Their names were Archibald, Bastian, and Cauldwell, and Harriet thought of them as Princes A, B, and C. She recognized them at once in spite of the masks. No one else had that same air of bored superiority.

She detested the princes cordially, because she had asked them for help long ago when the hamster kingdom had been trapped under a spell of sleep, and they had laughed at her. (Her mother insisted on the "cordial" part. Harriet would have preferred to detest them actively, possibly with screaming, but since their parents ruled neighboring kingdoms, this was not considered diplomatic.)

Harriet had been pretending that they did not exist all night. This was known in royal circles as "giving them the cut direct." Unfortunately, they hadn't noticed her, which is known in royal circles as "being oblivious."

Her mother showed up to talk to the bat ambassador. Harriet slouched off, looking for someone to talk to. Eventually she saw the only prince she really liked, her best friend Wilbur, who was lurking near the punch bowl. His mask was rather threadbare and could not hide his perpetually worried expression.

"Wilbur!" she said. "It's me!"

"That doesn't mean anything," said Harriet. "Lots of princesses walk like that."

Wilbur gave her a look. "Sure," he said. "And most of them have a sword stuffed under their ball gown too."

Harriet hastily adjusted her skirts to hide the sword, which was sticking out behind her like a long, slightly lopsided steel tail. "Yeah, well . . . I told Mom this wasn't going to work. What are you doing here? You don't like balls any more than I do."

"Ratpunzel wanted to come," said Wilbur. "She's never been to a ball before, so Mom asked me to come with her and make sure she was okay. Plus, the rat prince was going to be here, and she's still madly in love with him."

Harriet looked over to where Ratpunzel was dancing with a tall rat in a mask. She was imme-

diately identifiable by her enormously long tail, which she carried looped over her shoulder. She looked like she was having a great time.

"Well, I'm glad you're here. I was getting bored."

Wilbur did not reply. Wilbur appeared to have briefly lost the power of speech.

Harriet turned and followed his gaze. And blinked.

There was a hamster in a mask at the entrance to the ballroom. Her fur was gray, her dress was white, and she was absolutely stunning.

She was wearing shining glass slippers.

CHAPTER 3

Harriet did not often think about beauty, but she was generally considered a classic hamster beauty. She was round and fluffy, and her nose was perfectly twitchy and pink.

Being Harriet, she had worked hard to overcome this with interesting scars and a faint, lingering odor of quail, but was still at the very least quite lovely. It was just that people were generally too afraid to say so.

The hamster on the stairs, however, was in a class by herself. She looked like a small, fuzzy star. She had enormous eyes and eyelashes that could slice cheese. Her nose was orchid pink and her ears looked like tiny seashells. Her dress was studded with gems so that she seemed to move in a cloud of dazzling light. Her whiskers shone like spun glass thread.

She was so beautiful that the butler had forgotten how to announce her and was saying "Uh . . . the uh . . . the . . . a . . . Lady . . . uh . . ."

You couldn't even be jealous. It would be like being jealous of a sunset or a flower. She was beautiful in a way that seemed to have nothing at all to do with the person looking at her.

"Whoa," said Harriet.

"Who is *that?*" whispered Wilbur.

"I have no idea. I know all the princesses for miles around, and I don't know her. I'll ask." She made her way through the crowd to the new arrival.

The hamster girl was swept away by Prince A. Harriet blinked.

She tried again when that dance had ended a few minutes later. "Hi there! I'm—"

The rat who had been dancing with Ratpunzel cut in and pulled the hamster into a waltz.

Harriet raised her eyebrows.

The third time was the charm, and only because Prince B and Prince C both leaped to claim the stranger's hand for a dance and ran headlong into each other. (It is possible that Harriet's foot might have helped this along.)

"Come on," said Harriet, taking the stranger's arm. "You've been dancing all night. You need some punch."

"I—oh, I shouldn't!" A line formed between the hamster's eyes as she frowned. Even her frown was elegant. "I'm supposed to be here to meet princes . . ."

"I'll introduce you to the one by the punch bowl, then," said Harriet cheerfully. "His name's Wilbur. I'm sure he'd love to dance with you, but he's shy."

The stranger perked up. "I'd love to meet him!"

"Great!"

She steered the hamster in glass slippers to the punch bowl.

THIS IS MY FRIEND PRINCE WILBUR!

Harriet waited for a moment, and then, when it became obvious that Wilbur was not going to make anything but strangled gurgles, said, "He's pleased to meet you. What's your name?"

The stranger smiled through her beautiful whiskers. "It's a costume ball," she said. "I could be anyone."

And then, before Harriet could think of an answer to that—and before Wilbur could think of anything at all—another prince descended and swept the stranger off to dance.

CHAPTER 4

What gets me," said Harriet, a few hours later, sitting on a bale of hay in the stable, "is that not even Mom knew who she was. She wasn't on the guest list or anything. She crashed the bat ambassador's ball."

Harriet, Wilbur, and Ratpunzel had relocated to the stable. The castle was full of people running around cleaning up and lost party guests stumbling around trying to find their way to the bathroom or the exit (or both) and it was just easier to go down to the stables and get out of everyone's way. Plus it meant that Mumfrey, Harriet's beloved battle quail, could poke his head over the stall door and get his beak scratched.

"Was the ambassador mad?" asked Ratpunzel, round-eyed. She was a very sweet mouse who had grown up in near-total isolation, so people being angry upset her a great deal.

"No, no," said Harriet. "He thought it was

all hilarious. He thinks everything is hilarious, I think. No, what worries me is that we had an intruder and nobody noticed!"

"They certainly did notice," said Wilbur, scratching Mumfrey. "Everybody noticed her!"

"Qwerk," said Mumfrey, which was Quail for "A little to the left."

"Okay, okay," Harriet admitted, "once she came in, sure. But how did she *get* in? And how did she get out again before the unmasking?"

Because that was the crux of the mystery. At exactly midnight, everyone was supposed to take off their masks. Then, in theory, everyone would discover whom they had been dancing with, and there would be some hilarious misunderstandings and possibly a few unexpected romances.

In actual practice, everybody knew their friends (and enemies) perfectly well. To actually disguise

Harriet would have required a lot more than a small eye-mask. (She figured that she could do it with full-body bandages, like a mummy, if she only communicated in groans. She had gotten about three words into this suggestion before her mother had vetoed the entire thing.)

But at this ball, the real question was the identity of the mysterious and beautiful stranger—and she had vanished.

"Oh, that," said Ratpunzel. "She left about twenty minutes early. In a big round carriage pulled by two white quail."

"Qwerk?" said Mumfrey, suddenly interested.

"How do you know *that?*" asked Harriet.

"Um. I saw it?" said Ratpunzel. "One of the princes stepped on my tail and it got tangled up, so I had to go rewrap it."

"Is your tail okay?" asked Wilbur.

"Oh, yeah. You have people climb up and down a tower using your tail, you're not gonna care about the occasional foot." Ratpunzel patted her tail. "Anyway, I got lost trying to find the powder room—it's such a big castle!—and wound up in the tower."

Ratpunzel had lived almost all her life in only three rooms and got turned around easily in large buildings.

SO THEN IT WAS NEARLY MIDNIGHT, AND I FIGURED IT WAS GOING TO BE FASTER TO GO OUT THE WINDOW ON MY TAIL THAN FIND MY WAY BACK . . .

Harriet nodded. She approved of this sort of action.

"While I was out there I saw her come out of the castle and get in a carriage with white quail." Ratpunzel sat back. "And then I went inside, and we all unmasked and the rat prince danced with me again!"

WHITE QUAIL . . .
HMM . . .

"We could ask the grooms," said Wilbur. "They had to put the quail in the stables and bring them around for people. They're sure to remember white ones."

"Good idea!" Harriet slid off the hay bale and went to go find a groom.

WHITE QUAIL?
OH, AYE. THEY WENT INTO THE PADDOCK WITH THE OTHER GUEST QUAIL.

The groom frowned. "Odd sort of thing . . ." he added.

Harriet leaned forward. "What? What was odd?"

"Well . . . it was probably nothing, Princess . . ." The groom shifted nervously. "I don't want to get anyone in trouble."

"This goes no further," Harriet promised. "Nobody'll get in trouble."

"It was the fellow driving the coach with the white quail. Big white mouse in a hat with a plume. He parked the coach and then he just sat there on it."

"Now that *is* odd," said Wilbur.

"It is?" said Harriet, who did not know much about parking coaches.

"Well, think about it," said Wilbur. He had worked as a stableboy not that long ago and knew things that the usual sort of prince didn't know. "You park the coach and then you have to wait for the ball to be over so that you can take the prince or duke or whoever home, right? But who wants to sit on a coach for six or seven hours? So what usually happens is that you unhitch your quail so that they don't have to stand around waiting, and then you get down and go into the stable yourself and wait for the prince or the duke to call for you. Otherwise you're sitting around in the cold with nothing to do."

Ratpunzel blinked. "You mean he held it the whole time?"

Harriet did not really want to speculate on the bladder capacity of coach-mice. "Did he do anything else strange?"

"Well, he didn't talk to anybody," said the groom. "But there's some as are shy, and some as can't talk, so I didn't think much of that. But sitting on the coach all that time . . . that was odd."

Ratpunzel and Harriet and Wilbur looked at one another.

"Odd," said Harriet. "*Odd*. Yes."

"The ball's over, though," said Wilbur, "so I guess that's the end of that."

"Maybe," said Harriet. "But I still get the feeling we haven't seen the last of our mystery hamster. . . ."

CHAPTER 5

It took three days for Harriet to be proven correct, and it happened over breakfast.

"We must hold another ball!" said the hamster queen, just as Harriet was about to bite into her toast.

"Oh jeez," said Harriet. "Another one?"

"Yes," said the queen. "Prince Archibald's mother has been asking. They said there was a lovely masked hamster at the ball." She nudged Harriet and beamed. "Apparently all the princes are quite smitten!"

"Sure," said Harriet, "but not with me!"

Still, she couldn't be too annoyed. If the strange hamster showed up again, she'd have a second chance to get to the bottom of the mystery. And this time, she'd be prepared.

She went down to the stables and prowled around until she located the groom, who was shoveling quail manure.

"Sorry, Princess," he said, picking up his pitch-fork. "You startled me."

Harriet was used to people being startled when she showed up, and politely didn't comment.

"Can you help me . . . uh . . . sorry, what's your name?"

He looked at her warily. Princess Harriet had a reputation for danger and daring, and the groom was not particularly interested in either of those things.

MY NAME'S RALPH.

"Right!" said Harriet. "Ralph. Good. Now, we're going to have another masked ball shortly, and there's a chance that the coach with the white quail will show up again."

"Well, that's where I'll be," said Harriet. "I mean, I'd get away if I could, but my mom will notice, so I have to be there until I really need to leave."

"Princess, I'm a *groom*," said Ralph. "I can't go to a ball!"

"You'll be fine," said Harriet. "It's a costume ball. People will think you're a prince dressed as a groom!"

Ralph did not look thrilled by this prospect. Actually, if anything, he looked much more upset. "But if people think I'm a prince, they'll—they'll expect me to do prince things! Like dancing and—uh—table manners!"

Harriet snorted. "Believe me, most princes have no table manners at all. Anyway, it's not like you have to be there the whole time. You just have to come in and find me and then you can leave." She was a bit envious. She would have loved to spend the entire ball in the stables herself.

Ralph looked unconvinced. "Well . . . I guess . . . if I don't have to dance . . ."

"I shall protect you from dancing," said Harriet. "But it's very important that I see that coach and those quail!"

YES, PRINCESS HARRIET . . .

CHAPTER 6

The day of the ball arrived and Harriet was ready.

"You're really into this," said Wilbur, sitting on the edge of the bed. He and Ratpunzel were hanging out with Harriet before the ball started. Harriet's bedroom resembled an explosion in a weapons factory, so the bed was really the safest place. Otherwise you ran the risk of sitting down on an ax that had gotten wedged into the upholstery.

MYSTERIOUS MASKED
HAMSTERS SHOWING UP TO BALLS!
AREN'T YOU CURIOUS?

Wilbur shrugged. *"Everybody's* wearing a mask,"
he pointed out.

"It's probably just some local duchess or mar-
chioness or viscountess," said Ratpunzel.

Marchionesses and viscountesses are types of
female nobility, rather like duchesses, only lower
down on the social ladder. (For some reason,
though, female earls aren't earlesses, but count-
esses. Harriet suspected that it was because the
word "earless" looked like somebody who was
missing ears, not like somebody with a medium-
sized castle.)

Go far enough down the social ranks and people
are simply Lord So-and-So and Lady Such-and-
Such. There were a lot of lords and ladies about.
Some of them came to balls, but most of them
just lived ordinary lives. Being a lord didn't count

for much unless you inherited a castle and money to go with it.

"Or countess or baroness or knightess—" Ratpunzel continued, apparently determined to list every single type of nobility she knew.

"Female knights aren't knightesses," interrupted Harriet. "They're just knights."

"They aren't?" said Ratpunzel.

NOPE.
I'M A KNIGHT.
JUST A KNIGHT. SIR HARRIET. IF ANYBODY CALLED ME A KNIGHTESS, THEY'D LEARN THEIR MISTAKE.

"I thought female knights got called dame instead of sir," said Wilbur.

"They do, but I thought dame made it sound like I was eighty years old, so I said 'I want to be Sir Harriet instead' and they said 'Okay, that's fine, please go away now, you're scaring the chickens.'"

From Harriet's point of view, this was a perfectly normal conversation. Wilbur did not question it.

"Anyway," he said, "about the masked hamster . . ."

"Right!" said Harriet. "She can't have been anyone we know, because she didn't have an invitation! And Mom knows all the royalty for miles around, and *she* didn't know who it was!"

"Maybe she's not royalty at all," said Ratpunzel, combing her fur. "Maybe she just wanted to go to the ball."

"Blargggh," said Harriet. "Who'd want to go to a ball if they didn't have to?"

Wilbur and Ratpunzel exchanged glances. Ratpunzel was not the smartest rat in the kingdom, but even she knew that some people would very much want to go to balls, even if they weren't royal and didn't have an invitation.

"I would have loved to go to a ball when I was locked up in the tower," she said.

Harriet shuddered. "Yeah, but now you've seen what they're like," she said. "A bunch of people standing around punch bowls, dancing and worrying about stepping on each other's feet, and eating tiny little sandwiches with the crusts cut off."

I MEAN, THE SANDWICHES ARE PRETTY GOOD. IT'S JUST YOU NEED TO EAT LIKE THIRTY OF THEM TO GET FILLED UP.

"They can't be real glass," said Ratpunzel suddenly.

"What, the sandwiches? I think they're cucumber."

"No, no." Ratpunzel twisted her long tail between her hands. "The slippers! When you said that people stepped on each other's feet, I thought about her slippers. They can't be real glass."

It had not occurred to Harriet that anybody might think that the hamster's footwear was really made of glass. Real glass would have shattered into a million pieces and also been very, very uncomfortable to walk in.

"They must be magic," said Ratpunzel. "Don't you think?"

"Or some kind of transparent rubber." Harriet had a hard time imagining that, if you were a wizard or a fairy, you'd spend a lot of time magicking up shoes. There were so many more important things you could spend magic on, like swords or flying carpets or heavy artillery.

I JUST DON'T SEE THE POINT.

"I mean, have you *looked* at feet?" Harriet wiggled her toes. "They're all weird and knobbly. And if you shove them inside a slipper, they're all weird and knobbly with the toes squished together. And they'd be sweaty. And everybody could see your weird, squished sweaty feet whenever they looked down."

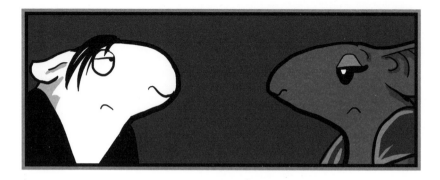

Fashion was not Harriet's strong suit.

The door at the bottom of the stairs opened, and Harriet's mother shouted, "Harriet! Time for the ball!"

"Right!" Harriet jumped out of the chair. "Come on, guys. And remember, whatever you do, when she arrives, don't let her out of your sight!"

CHAPTER 7

There was a herald stationed at the door to announce people, which was difficult when everyone was wearing masks and supposed to be anon-
ymous. Wilbur was announced as "Handsome
stranger!" Ratpunzel was "Exceedingly long-tailed
stranger!" Harriet was "Oh, it's you, Princess. Uh.
I mean, *Princess Stranger.*"

AND PRINCESSES
DON'T GET MUCH
STRANGER.

TOO EASY, WILBUR.
I KNOW YOU CAN DO
BETTER THAN THAT.

Wilbur sighed. He was not by nature a sarcastic hamster, but Harriet brought out some of his snarkier qualities. He still wasn't sure if that was a good thing.

The three of them drifted over to the punch bowl. Ratpunzel went off to dance with the rat prince. Wilbur ate several tiny sandwiches. Harriet kept an eye on the door, waiting for Ralph the groom.

When he finally arrived, he was out of breath and there was straw in his fur. The herald at the door looked him over and announced, "Stranger in a very convincing costume!"

Harriet hurried to meet him. "Ralph! It's me, Harriet!"

"Yes, Princess, I know," he said.

I TOLD MOM THIS WASN'T GOING TO WORK!

There was a moment when Ralph clearly realized that "Mom" meant "the hamster queen" and turned slightly green with social anxiety.

"Right!" said Harriet. "Is it the coach?"

"With the white quail. It just showed up!"

"Great!" said Harriet.

"I dunno, Princess," said Ralph. "Those quail aren't running right. I think they may have wobbly quail . . ."

(Wobbly quail is a terrible affliction of quail that requires extremely expensive orthopedic shoes to fix.)

Harriet winced. "Both of them? Are you sure?"

"Well, I don't rightly know. I told her about it and she seemed very concerned, but then I remembered that I was supposed to come here, and I'm sorry I took so long, but I was looking at the quail's feet . . ."

Harriet waved this off. "It's fine. Now we just have to—oh, blast!"

"Mysterious and beautiful stranger!" cried the herald at the front of the room.

The strange hamster swept into the room.

Her dress was the color of a summer sky. Her shoes were still made of glass. They also, now that Harriet was looking closely, were highly reflective, which resolved the issue of sweaty squished-up feet nicely.

She came down the steps into the ballroom. Princes, dukes, and minor nobility of all sorts rushed to dance with her. She looked across the room.

Ralph made a strangled noise.

I HELPED HER WITH HER COACH, PRINCESS! WE TALKED ABOUT WOBBLY QUAIL! SHE'LL RECOGNIZE ME!

Harriet nodded. Ralph did stick out, since he wasn't masked and nobody else had dressed up as a groom. The stranger might not notice it . . . but then again, she might, and it might make her ask inconvenient questions that would get Ralph in trouble. "I'll handle it," she whispered. "Get ready to go out the door!

"Hold this," she said, handing her punch to Wilbur, and advanced across the dance floor like a general advancing on the enemy.

Princes scattered before her. They did not have much choice in the matter.

Harriet reached the mysterious hamster, bowed as deeply as one can while wearing a ball gown, and said, "Madam, would you care to dance?"

CHAPTER 8

The stranger looked at her. Harriet looked at the stranger. She could feel the eyes of a great many princes on the back of her neck.

". . . sure," said the stranger, and took Harriet's hand.

Harriet was a large and sturdy hamster for twelve years old. The newcomer was at least sixteen or seventeen, but she was as delicate as a leaf, so they were at eye level to each other.

There was a moment or two of confusion when the stranger thought they were going to waltz and Harriet, panicking a little, defaulted to a tango. One glass slipper came down on Harriet's foot. It only hurt a little, but more important, it did not shatter into a million pieces. It felt hard and cold, not like rubber at all.

Magic glass, thought Harriet. *Ratpunzel and Wilbur were right.*

"You're not from around here," said Harriet.

"How would you know, Princess?" asked the stranger.

"The same way you knew I was a princess," said Harriet, which startled a laugh out of the stranger.

"What's your name?" asked Harriet.

"You may call me Ella," said the stranger.

"No last name?"

"Not that I'm going to tell you." She arched her beautiful whiskers forward smugly.

Harriet considered this. "Ella. With the whiskers. Whisker . . . Ella. Hmm."

WHISKERELLA! I LIKE THAT.

Harriet tried to spot Ralph over Whiskerella's shoulder, but they were pointing the wrong direction. She tried to spin the other way, which made Whiskerella stumble a bit and step on her foot again.

"You're a very . . . um . . . *unusual* . . . dancer," said Whiskerella.

"I'm better at jousting," admitted Harriet. "And cliff-diving. And fractions."

"Oh? What's three-eighths plus one-fourth?"

"Five-eighths," said Harriet.

"Your story checks out."

Harriet might have had a snarky reply, but then she saw Ralph, who was trying to get to the door but had run into Ratpunzel and was now helping her pick up her tail. "Oh blast!"

"Beg pardon?"

"Nothing. Let's go this way." Harriet steered them toward the back wall.

Other couples were moving in stately orbits like planets. Harriet and Whiskerella careened through them like a rogue comet.

"This is the most peculiar dance I've ever danced," said Whiskerella.

PEOPLE TELL ME I'M MEMORABLE. USUALLY I HAVE TO HIT THEM WITH A SWORD FIRST, THOUGH.

CAN WE SKIP THAT PART? I'M NOT DRESSED FOR IT.

Harriet managed to spin and saw Ralph run out the door. She breathed a sigh of relief. "Well, I don't want to keep you," she said. "And I'm sure lots of princes will want to dance with you."

"I doubt any of them will dance quite like you," said Whiskerella dryly. "At least, one can hope."

The music stopped. Couples bowed to each other, or curtseyed. Harriet bowed, remembered the ball gown, tried to curtsey, remembered the sword, and gave up. She stepped back.

Princes A, B, and C charged into the fray. Harriet waved to Whiskerella, then gathered up her skirts and ran for the door.

CHAPTER 9

She found Ralph having quiet hysterics in the hallway.

"Someone thought I was a prince!" he whispered.

"That *was* the idea," said Harriet.

"Yeah, but—but—she wanted to dance with me! She asked where I got my costume!" Ralph shuddered. "I don't know how to dance! I told her I had to go and ran away."

Harriet shook her head sadly. "You're too honest, Ralph. Tell people you have leprosy next time."

"Leprosy?!"

"Yeah, horrible disease, bits fall off, nobody wants to dance with you."

HAMSTER
WITH LEPROSY

———

(NOT TO BE
CONFUSED WITH
HAMSTER
MUMMY)

UNCLEAN

Ralph stopped and stared at her. Since Harriet was hurrying down the hallway, this meant that he stared at her back and then had to run to catch up. "I don't want to tell people I've got a horrible disease!"

"Fine, then tell them it's twenty-four-hour leprosy and you'll be better tomorrow."

They reached the stable yard. Ralph pointed toward the big paddock with the quail. "The white quail are in there, Har—err, Princess." (He was having a hard time remembering to call Harriet by her formal title. Harriet often had this effect on people.)

Harriet looked over, saw the white quail's topknots, and ran into the stable to deploy her secret weapon.

"Mumfrey!"

QWERK?

"Mumfrey!" whispered Harriet. "Mumfrey, go talk to those quail! See if you can find out where they're from!"

"Qwerk," said Mumfrey. He slicked his topknot back and went to go charm the two white quail.

"Qwerk," said Mumfrey, which was Quail for "So, you come here often?"

The white quail said nothing.

"Qwerkkkk," said Mumfrey, which was Quail for "Are you twins?"

The white quail continued to say nothing.

"Qwer-r-rk," said Mumfrey, which was Quail for "How about this weather we're having, huh?"

The white quail stared at him. If they had opinions of the weather, they kept it to themselves.

"Qwerrrrrk?" said Mumfrey, which was Quail for "So . . . uh . . . nice talking to you . . . ?"

The silence of the white quail seemed to chase him back into the stable.

"Well?" said Harriet. "What did they have to say?"

Mumfrey put his wing over his head. "Qwerk," he mumbled.

"Nothing?" said Harriet. "Not a word?"

"Qwerk."

This was very odd. Quail were among the chattiest birds in the world. Now they had two non-qwerking quail and Mumfrey was having an emotional crisis about whether he was likeable or not.

She hated to leave Mumfrey when he was obviously distraught, but the ball wouldn't last forever. "I have to go see the coach-mouse," she said. "I'll be back in just a minute."

"Qwerrrrrggggggk," mumbled Mumfrey into his wing.

Harriet made her way across the stable yard to where the coaches stood. For a very long ball, it was usual to park all the coaches and then unhitch the quail so that they didn't have to stand around for hours on end. The coaches sat empty in the moonlight with the shafts of the harness sticking out like fence posts.

Only one coach had anyone on it. It was a very old style of coach, at least a hundred years out of date, but Harriet was less concerned about the fashion and more about the coach-mouse sitting atop it.

He was small and white, with pink eyes and nose. He had a very large hat.

"I'm Princess Harriet!" said Harriet cheerfully. "What's your name?"

The coach-mouse stared at her.

Harriet was used to people staring at her in stunned silence. It seemed to happen a lot, in fact. She had gotten used to carrying the first part of the conversation. "Your coach has the white quail, right?"

The coach-mouse continued to stare.

After a moment it occurred to Harriet that he wasn't blinking. As soon as she realized that, her own eyes began to water in sympathy.

Harriet could think of any number of reasons why the coach-mouse wouldn't answer—he might be deaf or unable to speak or not speak Rodentish or simply painfully, agonizingly shy. None of those involved not blinking, however.

"Errr . . . are you doing okay?"

The coach-mouse didn't move a muscle. Harriet had to stop and wipe her watering eyes.

The coach-mouse did not reply, or move, or blink.

Harriet reached out a fingertip, very slowly, and touched the coach-mouse's shoe.

He exploded.

"GAAAH!" said Harriet. Whatever she'd been expecting, it wasn't that! She'd whacked people with swords, axes, frying pans, and, on one memorable occasion, an antique silver creamer in the shape of a cow, but she'd never made anyone explode just by touching them before.

She looked around wildly for bits of coachmouse, which was probably going to be very messy, but there was nothing. Just some rather glittery dust and, on top of the coach, a pile of clothes and . . .

. . . A LIZARD?

It was a rather small lizard with goggly eyes. It stared at her in exactly the same way that the coach-mouse had.

Harriet began to get a suspicion.

"Were you a lizard all along?" asked Harriet.

"Harriet?" called Wilbur. "What just happened? I saw a flash . . ."

Harriet turned her head to look for Wilbur and heard the scrabble of lizard feet. She whipped back around in time to see a tail vanishing over the side. "Blast!"

"I came out looking for you!" said Wilbur. "They're about to unmask!"

"I don't care about that," said Harriet. "I mean, Mom'll be mad, but—"

"No!" said Wilbur. "Not that! She left again! And she's calling for her coach!"

"There's magic going on!" said Harriet. "And we've got to get to the bottom of it!"

"Well, you've got about two minutes to do that,"

said Wilbur. "Because they're getting the quail out of the paddock now."

Harriet looked at Wilbur.

She looked at the pile of clothes that had recently been on an enchanted lizard.

She began to grin.

"Hey, Wilbur," she said. "Do you know how to drive a coach?"

CHAPTER 10

Harriet clung to the back of the coach with her teeth bared in a grin.

They were rattling down the road in the dark. The quail seemed to know the way to go, which was good, because Wilbur had no idea where they were headed.

He'd done great, though. Harriet had known he would. Wilbur was reliable that way.

With the hat pulled down over his small ears and the coach whip sticking out like a mouse's tail, he'd managed to pass as the coach-mouse. Nobody had really been looking at him, which helped. They were too busy staring at the beautiful stranger, and the stranger was too busy trying to get into the coach and away.

Harriet herself had grabbed on to the back of the coach and swung up onto it as it was leaving the courtyard. There was lots of trim on the coach—curving bits and curlicues and things carved to look like leaves and vines—so there were plenty of handholds. She just had to hang on.

The galloping quail began to slow down after a few minutes. Harriet recognized the turnoff to a nearby village. They hadn't gone very far at all, no more than a couple of miles.

The quail slowed to a walk and turned down a road, to a house set back in the trees.

Now we'll see where she lives, thought Harriet. *There can't be a grand manor house or a castle back here, can there? Somebody would have noticed . . . You can't just hide palaces around a corner in the village . . .*

It was not a manor house. It was a rather nice little two-story cottage with a thatched roof and a garden.

Harriet felt the coach coming to a stop and leaped down. She dove into the shrubbery before anyone could see her.

The door of the coach opened and Whiskerella got out. She looked tired and she was carrying her glass shoes in one hand.

"Good job, guys," she said to the quail, patting them on the shoulder. "You're really getting the hang of two legs."

As compliments went, this was decidedly odd.

"You too," she said over her shoulder to Wilbur. Wilbur wisely said nothing.

She opened the door of the cottage and went in.

Harriet glanced around the yard. It was neat and tidy, and nobody appeared to be watching. It wasn't the sort of place that had armed guards hanging around.

She was just about to sneak toward the coach when the clock tower in the village went:

BONG! BONG! BONG! BONG! BONG! BONG! BONG! BONG! BONG! BONG! BONG! BONG! BONG! BONG! BONG! BONG!

The coach exploded.

So did the quail.

It was a noiseless explosion, much like the coach-mouse. Glittering dust sprayed everywhere. The quail vanished and were replaced by a pair of newts. Wilbur let out a yelp and suddenly was sitting on top of a pumpkin.

"Hsst! Wilbur, over here!"

Wilbur looked around, determined that the voice was coming from the shrubs, and hurried to join Harriet. He looked like he was covered in silver flour.

"What. Just. *Happened?*" he demanded.

Harriet swiped a finger through the glitter and stuck it in her mouth. It tasted like spun sugar and dreams coming true and (faintly) like pumpkin.

FAIRY DUST. THOUGHT SO.

"I just got a wedgie from an enchanted vegetable!" snapped Wilbur. "That pumpkin stem went places!'

PLACES I *DO NOT WISH* TO HAVE PUMPKINS!

"Hazard of the job," said Harriet, slapping him on the back. Fairy dust rose in a cloud. They both coughed.

"So now what?" asked Wilbur.

"I want to know whose house this is," said Harriet. "There's a fairy at work here, and they're spending a lot of magic. Look at all this dust!"

They looked at the house. It continued to be dark. The two newts who had previously been quail curled up in one corner of the yard and began to snore.

"Errr . . . are we gonna be here for a while?"

asked Wilbur. "Because I have a philosophical objection to lurking in a stranger's shrubberies. People catch you lurking in shrubberies and they think you're a weirdo."

"You are not cut out for adventure, Wilbur," said Harriet. "Lurking in strange shrubberies is like half the job. Possibly two-thirds." She chewed on her lower lip. "Hmm, maybe not quite that. Nine-sixteenths, let's say . . ."

NO FRACTIONS
AT THIS HOUR OF THE NIGHT.
PLEASE.

The snoring changed in volume as the newts rolled over.

"Maybe she'll come back out," said Harriet.

"Maybe she's *tired*," said Wilbur. "She was dancing for half the night. *I'm* tired, and I mostly stood by the punch bowl."

"Fine," said Harriet. "We'll try the direct approach." She climbed out of the shrubberies, crossed the yard, and knocked on the door.

CHAPTER 11

It took a few minutes for anyone to answer. Harriet had to knock again, and was about to start banging on the door in earnest when it opened.

It was Whiskerella, but it took Harriet a moment to recognize her.

She wasn't wearing a mask. She wasn't wearing glass slippers or a ball gown. She had on an old bathrobe and she looked tired.

And she wasn't . . .

Well, she wasn't . . .

"You're not beautiful!" blurted Harriet.

"And you're not tactful, Princess," said Whiskerella dryly. "I can maybe do something with my hair, but I think you're stuck."

HARRIET!

"Sorry," said Harriet. "I mean—um—you're very pretty. Still. That didn't come out right. I mean—that is—"

Whiskerella shook her head. "Quit while you're ahead," she suggested. "And come inside."

They followed Whiskerella into the cottage. Wilbur elbowed Harriet. "That was rude!" he hissed.

"I'm sorry!" whispered Harriet. "Really! I just—I wasn't expecting—"

Because the truth was that Whiskerella was still a very pretty hamster . . . but only pretty. The strange, otherworldly gorgeousness that had hovered around her at the ball was gone. Her fur was the soft gray of dusty velvet, not of clouds, and the sparkle in her eyes was like crystal, not like diamond.

Whiskerella led them into the kitchen. "Pull up a chair, Your Highnesses," she suggested. "I'll make some tea."

"No Highnessing," said Harriet. *"Please."* She and Wilbur sat down at the table.

Whiskerella looked doubtful.

"Look, you've met the princes," said Harriet. "Royalty isn't what it's cracked up to be." Whiskerella laughed and seemed to relax.

It was a nice little kitchen. It was warm and cozy, even at night.

WELL, YOU'VE FIGURED OUT MY SECRET. I'M NOT A PRINCESS. AND I'M NOT PARTICULARLY BEAUTIFUL.

"You're plenty beautiful," said Wilbur gallantly.

"That's sweet of you to say," said Whiskerella. "But it's not the same without the mask and the enchanted slippers. When I have those on, I'm beautiful. *Magically* beautiful."

"There's a fairy involved, isn't there?" said Harriet.

ELLA?
IS SOMEONE
HERE?

Harriet and Wilbur turned to the new arrival. She was a bit older than Whiskerella and looked as if she'd just woken up.

"Yes, Misty," said Whiskerella. She held out her hand to the newcomer. "This is Princess Harriet and Prince Wilbur, from the palace."

"Oh dear," said Misty. She sat down at the table. "Have they come because of the business?"

"What business?" asked Wilbur.

"Fairy business," said Whiskerella. "Harriet's right."

"But who are you?" asked Wilbur. "You're not a fairy!"

"Oh dear, no!" Misty laughed.

CHAPTER 12

I'm afraid there's only one of me," said Misty apologetically. "I know there's supposed to be two stepsisters. But I try to make up for it by being especially wicked."

Whiskerella rolled her eyes. "You're about as wicked as a cinnamon roll." Misty giggled.

"A wicked stepsister," said Harriet thoughtfully. "And a fairy who turns your newts into coach-quail . . . You don't have a wicked stepmother too, by any chance?"

"Oh, dreadfully wicked," said Misty, giggling harder. "A regular monster!"

Whiskerella groaned.

Whiskerella put her head in her hands. "Right.
Well, it all started a few weeks ago . . ."

100

101

... WHAT JUST HAPPENED?

She waved her hands in the air. "And the next thing I knew, she was turning my clothes into ball gowns and I had glass slippers and the poor newts were turned into quail and Misty's lizard, Stinky, was turned into a mouse!"

"I offered to go," said Misty. "I'm already a mouse. But apparently it was enchantment or nothing. Where *is* Stinky, anyway?"

Misty looked worried for the first time. "Oh dear! We should probably find him. He widdles when he gets nervous."

OH ...
UH ... YEAH ...
HIM ... I THINK
HE'S STILL AT THE
PALACE ...

Harriet thought that she could have handled a fairy. She could have handled the enchantments, and Whiskerella's not-particularly-wicked stepsister, and the glass slippers. These were properly heroic things for a hero who was also a princess to deal with.

A widdling lizard named Stinky, however, was just too much. Heroes could not be expected to work under these conditions. She rubbed her hands over her face.

"It's his bladder, you understand," said Misty. "He's not as young as he used to be."

"Let's focus on the fairy for a minute," said Wilbur, glancing worriedly at Harriet. "I'm sure Stinky will turn up."

"Right. Well, thought maybe it was just one of those things that happens," said Whiskerella glumly. "Mistaken identity or something. I don't know why I'd need a fairy godmouse."

"Fairy godmice are notorious do-gooders," said Harriet. "They will do good at anything that can't run away. Sometimes it's best to just get it over with. I had three." She looked gloomily into her teacup. "One of them did a spell to cover the castle in huge thorns. Dad is still mad about that."

"No thorns," said Whiskerella. "Just pumpkins. And she turned poor Stinky into a mouse! And

the newts—Webby and Wubby, they're sisters—
she turned them into quail. They were so confused."

SHE MADE THIS
GORGEOUS DRESS, THOUGH.
I TOLD ELLA SHE SHOULD GO
TO THE BALL.

"So I did," said Whiskerella. "I put on the shoes,
and suddenly I was spectacularly beautiful. And
that's when it started to go wrong."

CHAPTER 13

It was fun, the first time." She gave Harriet a defiant look. "All those princes wanting to dance with me, when I knew they'd never look at me in real life."

OH, C'MON,
ALL PRINCES AREN'T
THAT SHALLOW . . .

Wilbur sighed.

"But then it got weird," Whiskerella continued. "I didn't expect there to be a second ball! I went to take the trash out yesterday evening and there was this POOF and fairy dust everywhere and there was the coach and the quail and poor Stinky in a hat!"

"He widdled *everywhere*," said Misty.

"And then at the ball—one of the princes proposed to me! And another started talking about engagement rings!"

"Yeesh," said Harriet.

"I suppose you don't want to marry any of them?" said Wilbur.

"No! And even if I did, what do you think would happen when I took the magic shoes off and wasn't beautiful anymore?"

Harriet winced. She couldn't imagine one of the princes A, B, or C being understanding about that sort of thing.

ANYWAY, THE IMPORTANT THING IS THAT IT'S OVER NOW. I WENT TO THE BALL, IT WAS FUN, WE'LL GO GET STINKY TOMORROW AND EVERYTHING'LL GO BACK TO NORMAL.

... UH. YEAH. ABOUT THAT ...

"Fairy curses don't work like that," said Harriet apologetically. "I mean, not that this was meant as a curse, I guess it was supposed to be a gift, but it's basically the same thing. All fairy magic is basically alike, whether the fairies are trying to be nice or not. If she said you're going to the ball and going to meet a handsome prince who will sweep you off your feet, then . . . well . . . that's what's going to happen. And keep *on* happening. Whether you want it to or not."

"You'll be going to balls until you meet that prince or you die of old age," said Wilbur. "I mean, possibly you can't even die of old age until you meet him. You might not even age. Fairy magic is *weird*."

"Ooh!" said Harriet. "That'd be awesome! You could be totally immortal and like a thousand years old, as long as you keep going to balls every now and then!"

She waved her bare foot in Harriet's direction. Her toes were red and starting to blister. "My toes will fall off!"

Harriet considered this. "Okay, yeah, immortality where you have to keep going to balls would be pretty annoying. The cucumber sandwiches aren't *that* good. Plus the feet-falling-off thing."

"Particularly if I have to keep dancing with princes!" Whiskerella put her face in her hands and groaned. "They all seemed awful. They kept telling me how wonderful they were compared to the other princes. Except for the rat prince, but I don't think he was really interested in me."

"He's hopelessly in love with Ratpunzel," said Harriet. "It's cool."

THE ONLY PERSON I MET WHO WAS ACTUALLY *NICE*—NOT JUST POLITE—WAS THE GROOM WHO TOOK THE COACH.

"He was worried about the newts," she said. "Because they're not good at running on two legs. He thought they had something called 'wobbly quail.' And he asked about poor Stinky. He kept saying he didn't have to sit on the coach this time, he could come inside with everybody else and if he was shy, that was fine, he didn't have to talk. He could just have some cider, he didn't have to stay outside in the cold."

She leaned back in her chair. "But then he actually looked at me and he suddenly got all tongue-tied and ran away."

Wilbur and Harriet exchanged looks. There was only one groom who fit that description.

". . . You mean *Ralph?*"

CHAPTER 14

Well, this is a problem," said Harriet as she and Wilbur trudged up the road toward the castle.

"You mean the fact that we've stayed out half the night and missed our bedtime, curfew, and, at this rate, probably breakfast?"

"What?" said Harriet. "I stay out all the time."

"Is your mom afraid something will happen to you?"

"*I*," said Harriet, with absolute confidence, "am something that happens to *other* people."

Wilbur nodded. This was undeniably true.

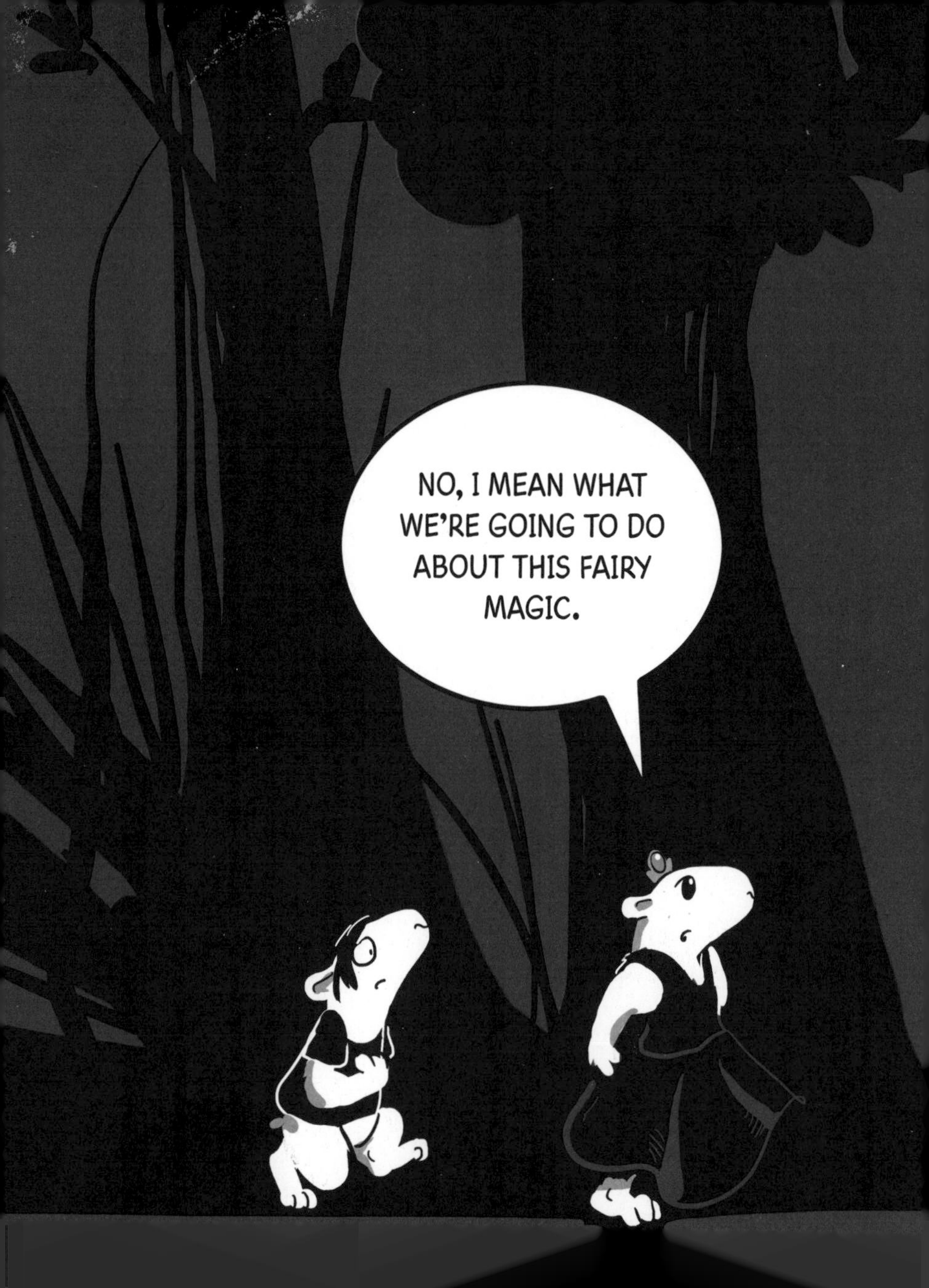
NO, I MEAN WHAT WE'RE GOING TO DO ABOUT THIS FAIRY MAGIC.

"We're gonna have to find a prince to sweep Whiskerella off her feet." She scowled. "It's a shame we can't make Ralph a prince."

Wilbur rubbed his forehead. Harriet was a great warrior, a fantastic quail rider, a skilled cliff-diver, and a good friend. As a matchmaker, however, she left a lot to be desired. "They've talked once. About wobbly quail. And then he panicked and ran away."

QUAIL DISEASES ARE NOT A SOLID FOUNDATION FOR A RELATIONSHIP!

I WOULD DATE SOMEONE WHO TALKED TO ME ABOUT QUAIL DISEASES.

YES, BUT YOU'RE . . .

Wilbur floundered for a way to finish that sentence, and eventually settled on *". . . you."*

"Quail diseases are important, Wilbur. Have you ever seen a quail with bent gizzard?"

"Will bent gizzard get us any closer to breaking this fairy magic?"

"Fine, fine . . ." Harriet sighed. "We can't make Ralph a prince anyway. He's older than either of us."

". . . say again?" said Wilbur.

"Okay, look," said Harriet. "This is really straightforward. Kings and queens have princes and princesses for kids, right?"

"I am with you so far," said Wilbur.

"And the oldest prince or princess becomes the king or the queen when their parents either die or retire, right?" (Harriet's grandfather had retired and taken up fishing and now lived in the far north, where he said that the ice fishing was excellent and much better than having to run a country.)

"Okay," said Wilbur.

"Ralph is older than either of us," Harriet repeated.

"Okay . . . ?"

SO WE CAN'T JUST HAVE MY PARENTS ADOPT HIM! HE'D BECOME THE KING INSTEAD OF ME! AND IF YOUR MOM ADOPTS HIM, HE'D BE KING INSTEAD OF YOU!

"I wouldn't do that to him," said Wilbur gloomily. "It would be awful to inherit our castle. The moat's leaking and the furnace has been making weird noises."

They walked along in silence for a while. Crickets chirped in the woods. Harriet stared up at the sky through the trees. The moon was pale and distant and shone almost like a glass slipper.

"Okay," said Harriet, ticking off plans on her fingers. "Let's see. We'll need to throw another ball, and then I'll go along with Whiskerella and see if I can't find this fairy godmouse of hers and get a few things straight."

"And find Stinky," added Wilbur.

"Right, and find Stinky." Harriet pictured a nervous lizard widdling all over the palace and shuddered. "In fact, we should try to find Stinky *first*."

Wilbur yawned and put a hand over his mouth.

"Do you think we could go to bed first? I'm really tired and it's so late it's practically early. I'm not going to be good for much when we get back."

"But he could widdle on things, Wilbur! On *all* the things!"

THINK OF THE WIDDLE, WILBUR!

"I beg your pardon," said a cultured voice from overhead, "but can I be of some assistance?"

CHAPTER 15

It was the bat ambassador.

He dropped out of the sky and landed in front of them as easily as Harriet might sit down in a chair. His feet weren't much good for walking on, so he braced himself up on his wings. This made him rather shorter than Harriet and Wilbur, but it didn't seem to bother him much.

Harriet bowed. The ambassador dipped his head in return. Wilbur looked from one to the other and said, "Errr . . . uh . . . oh! Right!" and bowed as well.

To the ambassador's credit, he did not ask questions like "Why are you looking for a lizard with a bladder problem?" For an adult, the ambassador seemed very sensible.

"I see," he said. "Perhaps I can help. I will scout the outside of the castle and see if I can find him for you."

"That would be really helpful," said Harriet gratefully. "He's probably a bit freaked out. And covered in fairy dust."

FAIRY DUST! MY GOODNESS! WHAT DOES THAT LOOK LIKE?

"Sort of like glittery flour," said Harriet. "Gets into everything."

"Fascinating," said the bat. "We don't have fairies in my country, I'm afraid."

"There aren't any bat fairies?"

"No, indeed. We have witches and banshees and cunning-folk—and vampires, of course—but no fairies."

VAMPIRES?!

AH, YES. A SAD AFFLICTION. MOST OF THEM LIVE ON RAW STEAK AND ENERGY DRINKS, BUT A FEW GO BAD AND BEGIN DRINKING PEOPLE'S BLOOD.

"Rather like your Ogrecats, I believe."

Harriet nodded. Ogrecats could live on seafood and soy protein, but some of them didn't want to. It was occasionally Harriet's job to go around and explain why eating the neighbors was frowned upon in civilized society, and then to hit them repeatedly with a sword until they understood the explanation.

"Well, we've got fairies," she said. "They give people magical gifts and sometimes it's great—I can cliff-dive from anywhere!—and sometimes it's terrible. Like poor Whiskerella got cursed to go to the ball in pinchy glass slippers and a pumpkin coach. With a lizard."

"Named Stinky," said Wilbur.

"Hopefully I can catch the fairy and talk to her," said Harriet. "But we'll need to hold *another* ball so she shows up."

She clutched her forehead in both hands. The idea of even more dancing was grueling.

The bat ambassador made a high, chattering sound that startled both Wilbur and Harriet, until they realized that he was laughing. "Another ball! Well, perhaps I can help with that too. But first, let us find your lizard before his bladder suffers too greatly . . ."

He leaped into the air, flapping his wings, and was immediately airborne. He swooped once past their heads, then winged his way into the darkness.

CHAPTER 16

As it turned out, finding Stinky wasn't the problem. They found him on three separate occasions.

Catching him was another matter.

Stinky was fast. And nervous. And slippery with something that Harriet desperately hoped was slime and not something of a more widdle-some nature.

"I give up," said Wilbur as Stinky bolted past them for the third time, vanishing into a pipe. Harriet lunged after the lizard and jammed her arm in the pipe. Her fingers just brushed his tail.

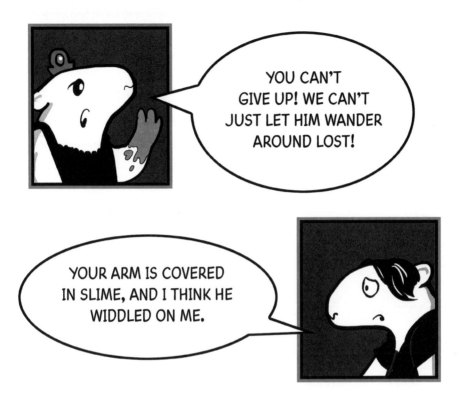

"He could widdle on everything! My mother will lose her mind! I'm not even allowed to have newts inside the castle!"

"I'm sorry," said the bat ambassador, clinging to the side of the tower. He looked apologetic. "I fear he is easily located, but not easily trapped."

"Do you have lizards in your country?" asked Harriet, interested.

"Yes, but they are as large as your quail. We use them as beasts of burden. For small pets, like your newts, we keep moths instead. They assist us in hunting insects."

"Fascinating as all this is," said Wilbur, "I'm going to bed. I have to get up in like three hours."

"But Stinky!"

"Stinky will still be here tomorrow," said Wilbur. "I have absolutely no doubt that Stinky is in no danger from predators. I don't think a predator could get within twenty yards of him."

"But—!"

Wilbur gave Harriet a Look and went into the castle. Harriet sighed.

"I too must roost," said the bat ambassador. He stifled a yawn behind his wing-claws. "As entertaining as hunting such an . . . *interesting* . . . lizard has been, it is nearly morning, and we bats must sleep during the day."

"Well, maybe he'll turn up," said Harriet with a sigh. She had to admit that she was getting a little tired herself, and also her ball gown had been through rather a lot this evening. It had not been designed for clinging to the backs of carriages, fairy dust explosions, hunting lizards, and multiple trips through the stable yard.

... MOM IS GONNA KILL ME.

"Oh, I doubt that," said the bat ambassador cheerfully. "She seems like a lovely hamster. A most gracious host."

"It's different when she's your mom," said Harriet.

"Very true," said the ambassador gravely. "It has been a pleasure, Princess. Good luck with your lizard."

Harriet waved to him and followed Wilbur into the castle.

She slept late that morning, and didn't wake up until her mother came into the bedroom.

"It was only a little slime," said Harriet, sitting up. "Hardly any. A dress that can't handle slime is a stupid dress."

The hamster queen had known Harriet for her daughter's entire life, and so she did not bother trying to explain the finer points of clothing. Nor did she try to find out where the slime had come from. The hamster queen was a firm believer that a little carefully applied ignorance made parenting easier for everyone.

Instead she said, "You'll need a new dress."

"What? Why?"

"For the bat ambassador's ball." She clasped her hands together. "He said that he enjoyed the last two so much that he would like to throw another one here. He's overseeing all the arrangements, though, so that your father and I can come to the ball as guests instead of worrying about everything. Isn't that nice of him?"

"Definitely!" said Harriet, although for slightly different reasons. The ambassador really had helped her. For a grown-up, he was *very* cool. Now she just had to find a way to sneak out and catch the fairy in the act, and save Whiskerella from a life of never-ending dances and cucumber sandwiches.

"I'm looking forward to it so much," said her mother happily.

YOU KNOW?
SO AM I...

Astonished by how agreeable her daughter was being, the hamster queen practically spun out of the room.

CHAPTER 17

Preparation for the ball hit a snag the next day.

"Harriet," said her mother, in a dangerously calm voice, "did you let one of the newts sleep in the castle with you?"

"A newt?" Harriet was baffled. "No. I have not done that since I was like seven and you yelled at me for sneaking tadpoles from the kennel."

"Are you certain?" asked her mother. "Because someone has widdled in the hallway. *In three places.*"

"Are you sure it's not lizard widdle, instead of newt?"

Her mother looked down her snout at Harriet. "Is there any particular *reason* you would suspect a lizard?"

Harriet did several mental calculations, and all of them involved many more explana-tions than she wanted to make. "Errr . . . asking for a friend?

"Annnnyway," said Harriet hurriedly. "When's the ball?"

"Two days," said the hamster queen. "I have had a replacement dress made since you managed to destroy the last one."

Harriet groaned. "Can't I just wear my usual clothes?"

"No. The bat ambassador will think you're being disrespectful, after all his effort. It would be an international incident."

Privately Harriet thought that the bat ambassador would think it was hilarious, but this didn't seem to be the time.

Two days, she thought. Her mother was talking about something, so she smiled and nodded. *Two days. I'll go down to Whiskerella's house and lie in wait for the fairy. She has to come out for the ball.*

She wasn't quite sure what she'd do once she encountered the fairy. Convince her that what she was doing was wrong? Whack her repeatedly with a sword? Harriet was a firm believer in improvisation.

The biggest problem, ultimately, was getting out of the castle right before the ball. Sneaking out was easy, but Harriet's mother was going to come looking for her right before the ball to make sure that she actually showed up.

Harriet knew that she couldn't do it alone, and she also knew that she wanted Wilbur with her. Wilbur was very reliable in his own way, even if he wasn't really cut out to be a warrior.

That left one person to carry out the deception back at the castle.

YOU WANT ME TO PRETEND YOU'RE IN THE *BATHROOM?*

"Yes," said Harriet. "Look, it's very simple. If anybody asks, I just stepped into the bathroom to—err—powder my ears. You just saw me a minute ago."

Ratpunzel did not have a skeptical bone in her body. She twisted her tail in her paws and said, "Well . . . okay . . . but isn't your mom going to think you've been in the bathroom for a long time?"

"Tell her I'm afraid I'll widdle in the hall," said Harriet, and hurried off to find Wilbur.

CHAPTER 18

Harriet met Wilbur an hour before the ball was due to start. They climbed down Ratpunzel's tail, out of the window, and scurried into the bushes before anyone could see them.

"This would be faster if we could take the quail," said Wilbur glumly.

"Yeah, but the stable hands know to get Mom if I try to ride Mumfrey out before a ball." Harriet sighed. She had tried to escape dancing a few too many times in the past, and now it had caught up with her. They were going to have to walk to Whis-kerella's house.

"It's a shame we can't take Heady," said Har-riet. (Heady was Mumfrey's hydra friend.)

"She's helping cook for the ball. They'll *definitely* notice if she goes missing."

"Oh, well . . ."

They scurried down the road toward the village. Whenever a coach went by, they had to dive into the bushes in case it was someone going to the ball.

By the time they reached the cottage, they were both covered in leaves and bits of twig. Whiskerella came out to meet them.

"Did you fall into a forest?" asked Whiskerella.

"New fashion," said Harriet cheerfully. "Twig chic." She dusted herself off as best she could. "Is the fairy here yet?"

"No," said Whiskerella hopefully. "Maybe she won't show up?"

I DOUBT WE'LL BE SO LUCKY. FAIRIES ARE REALLY SINGLE-MINDED ONCE THEY GET THEIR CLAWS IN YOU.

"Why are you helping me, anyway?" asked Whiskerella abruptly.

Harriet looked at her blankly. "What?"

"You're helping me. You're stopping this fairy. Why?"

ERR ...
DON'T YOU WANT
HELP?

YES!
BUT WHY DO YOU
WANT TO HELP?

Harriet spread her hands. "Have you *seen* those princes? Nobody should have to marry one of those guys!"

The other hamster groaned. "I kept trying to be nice, hoping they'd be less awful. But they were like . . . awful all the way through!"

"Like onions," agreed Harriet. "You keep peeling off layers and yup, *still* an onion. Only . . . y'know . . . with awfulness instead of onion."

Whiskerella had the briefly stunned look that many people wore when hit with one of Harriet's metaphors. Harriet carried on. "Anyway, your mom builds hospitals for sick mice. *I* couldn't do that. But she's trying to make the world a better place, and so am I."

PREFERABLY BY HITTING THINGS WITH SWORDS, CLIFF-DIVING, AND OCCASIONALLY BREAKING FAIRY CURSES.

Misty came out of the cottage with three mugs of cider and handed one to Harriet. "I hope she lets me come along as the coach-mouse this time . . ."

"If she doesn't, come up tomorrow," suggested Harriet. "Maybe Stinky will come out if he sees you there."

"I hope so," said Misty. "I'm worried about him."

"Judging by the quantity of widdle, he's doing fine."

Misty opened her mouth to say something but was cut off by a sound.

It was a very strange sound. It was the noise that glitter would make if glitter made a noise. It went:

It was the sound of fairy magic.

Light sprouted up from the ground and fell back down in shimmering bands of fairy dust. A figure formed in the heart of the light, swathed in magic.

Whiskerella winced. Harriet grabbed for her sword.

"Hello, my dearrrr!" sang a voice. "I've come to help you yet again!"

"Halt!" cried Harriet. "She's not going to the ball!"

CHAPTER 19

The fairy looked at her. She was a plump, jolly mouse with twinkling eyes, tiny wings, and a wand with a star on it, and Harriet suspected that she could turn violent in an instant.

"And who might you be, my dearrr?" asked the fairy, rolling her *R*s magnificently.

"I'm Princess Harriet Hamsterbone, and I'm here to save Whiskerella." She eyed the wand. It looked loaded. "She doesn't want to go to balls anymore. She's not interested in any of the princes."

"Nonsense," said the fairy, and even though there weren't any *R*s in *nonsense*, she somehow managed to roll the ones that weren't there.

"Tell her, Whiskerella!" said Harriet.

"Eh?" Whiskerella was watching them with a bemused expression. "I don't know anything about vampires . . ."

"About the princes!"

"Oh, them." Whiskerella made a face. "They're awful. Except Wilbur, he's fine. But I don't want to marry him."

The fairy godmouse was starting to look less jolly and more irate. "I've given you a grand opportunity to go to the ball and marry far above your station, and you're complaining about it?"

I GAVE YOU A MAGIC DRESS AND GLASS SLIPPERS AND TURNED A PUMPKIN INTO A COACH FOR YOU . . .

AND NOW THESE PRINCES *AREN'T GOOD ENOUGH FOR YOU?*

Harriet noticed that she'd stopped rolling her Rs. This seemed like a bad sign.

"It's not that they aren't good enough!" said Whiskerella hurriedly. "I'm very grateful! It's just—uh—I'm not really feeling an emotional connection—"

"No, they're *not* good enough," said Harriet. "I mean, have you met the princes A, B, and C? They're dreadful. Whiskerella's worth ten of them. Put together."

The fairy wheeled on her. "This is your fault!"

NO IT ISN—
UH. WELL, OKAY,
YES, TECHNICALLY
IT IS, BUT—

"Interfering wretch! I heard about what you did to poor Ratshade!" cried the fairy.

"Poor Ratshade?" Harriet grabbed for her sword. "She cursed me! I was an infant!"

"And instead of being saved by a prince like a normal person, you threw her into a hamster wheel and chopped her magic off!"

"And I'd do it again!" shouted Harriet.

Wilbur leaned over to Misty and said, in an undertone, "I think negotiation has gone off the rails."

The fairy was seething. The twinkle in her eyes had been replaced with a gleam. "Well, you're not wrecking *this* fairy's magic," she said. "Whiskerella *will* go to the ball!"

NOT WITH STINKY!

EH? WHAT?
DID YOU SAY SOMETHING,
WICKED STEPSISTER?

"My name is Misty," said Misty. "And you turned my pet lizard, Stinky, into a coach-mouse, even though I offered to go instead. And now he's gotten lost up at the castle and he's widdling on tapestries, so you can't turn him into a coach-mouse. And I think he's well out of it!"

The fairy godmouse blinked at her. Misty folded her arms and glared.

"Well, there you go," said Wilbur hurriedly. "No coach-mouse, no luck. And there's no newts to turn into quail, either."

The fairy spun around to face him. "What happened to the newts?"

"Wobbly quail," said Whiskerella grimly. "Which newts aren't even supposed to get, but you turned them into quail, and now they're at the vet getting fitted for orthopedic shoes. I'm a little annoyed about that, let me tell you!"

"I don't think being dead is going to make me very happy—" Whiskerella started to say.

And then she stopped.

All four of them stopped. Harriet tried to move, tried to speak, and discovered that she was frozen in place.

The fairy held up her wand. The star at the end had begun to glow.

CHAPTER 20

Do you think it's easy being a fairy?" ranted the fairy godmouse. "No! It isn't! Not when the world is full of ungrateful people who won't be happy!"

All Harriet could move were her eyes. She looked over at Wilbur, then at Misty and Whiskerella. Nobody had so much as blinked.

"No dress? Fine!" The fairy waved her wand over Whiskerella.

A glorious dress shot up from the ground and wrapped itself around Whiskerella. The glass slippers snapped over her feet like manacles. As soon as they touched her toes, she was terribly, tragically beautiful again, the sort of beauty that people write very bad poems about.

She couldn't talk, but it was clear from her wince that the shoes were still pinching her toes.

"No lizard? Fine!" The fairy pointed her wand at Misty.

Misty was suddenly clad in the coach-mouse's gear, with the hat sliding down over one eye.

"You'll drive the coach," said the fairy. "So I suppose I should let you move. But no talking. I'm not going to let your wickedness get in the way of Whiskerella's happiness!"

Misty opened and closed her mouth a few times, but no sound came out. Whiskerella, encased in the dress and slippers, looked furious. The tips of her ears were turning scarlet with rage. Her magnificent whiskers quivered.

She managed to stamp her slippered foot and it made a high chiming sound, like glasses clinking together.

"Temper, temper," said the fairy godmouse. "No breaking that slipper until after the ball! We wouldn't want that spell to end early, now would we?"

She turned to Wilbur and Harriet. Wilbur was grinding his teeth and Harriet was trying (unsuccessfully) to reach her sword.

She slapped her wand into her hand.
"Oh, *wait.*"

POOF-POOF!

Harriet felt warm. Then she felt hot. Then she felt her neck doing something that necks are not supposed to do. It didn't hurt, it was just strange and stretchy, and her hands seemed to be getting very long and strange, and so did her legs, and her lips were suddenly very long and also very stiff and . . .

She turned her head to look at Wilbur, but Wilbur wasn't there.

Instead, there was a short, forlorn white quail standing next to her. She could tell it was Wilbur because he still had a shock of black feathers flopping down over his eyes.

"Holy mackerel," she tried to say. "We've been turned into quail!"

Instead what she said was: "Qwerk!"

"That's right," said the fairy. "And nobody who isn't a quail is going to understand a word you say . . ."

This was Quail for "It's okay. It'll be fine. We'll sort this out."

"But I don't wanna be a quail!" qwerked Wilbur in Quail.

"I'm sure it's only temporary!" qwerked Harriet.

It occurred to her that being a quail was not the worst thing she could be. She was now extremely strong, extremely fast, and capable of—if not exactly flight, at least a pretty solid flapping glide. And while she didn't have thumbs, she now had a truly ferocious kick.

She turned toward the fairy godmother.

"Let them go!" cried Whiskerella. "Let them go! I'll go to the ball, just turn them back and make my sister talk again!"

"No!" qwerked Harriet, but Whiskerella didn't seem to understand her.

"You should have thought of that before," said the fairy. "But I'll be happy to turn them back . . ."

"Now for the coach!" she said, and snapped her fingers.

Harriet lunged forward, preparing to give the fairy a kicking that she wouldn't forget in a hurry, but it was too late.

"Naughty quail!" said the fairy. The pumpkin coach exploded into existence, and a harness dropped over Harriet's shoulders, or what passed for shoulders on a quail. There was suddenly a bridle around her beak, and then she ran into the end of the harness and dragged the coach (and Wilbur) several feet forward. Wilbur let out a squawk and nearly fell over.

"Get in," said the fairy to Whiskerella. "The

ball's about to start, and the sooner you get there, the sooner you'll be swept off your feet."

"W-won't the magic wear off at midnight again?" asked Whiskerella.

The fairy grinned wickedly. "Oh no. This time I've got something special planned. Something to keep all these people from meddling with the happy ending. No prince, no turning back from being quail! Now get in!"

Whiskerella gave Wilbur and Harriet a panicked look. Harriet dipped her head and qwerked in what she hoped was a comforting fashion.

Misty climbed onto the coach. She had no idea what to do with the reins, but that was fine. Harriet had a plan. Well . . . part of a plan.

Well . . . something definitely plan-shaped, anyway.

Harriet stepped forward. Wilbur didn't. The carriage fishtailed. Harriet stopped. Wilbur started. The carriage swerved in the other direction and shuddered to a halt.

Harriet wondered how long it had taken the newts to figure it out the first time. She'd hate to be worse at something than a transfigured newt.

"Okay," she qwerked to Wilbur. "Left foot first. And . . . left, right, left right left . . ."

It took them a few moments to get their feet matched. In stops and starts, lunges and lurches, they pulled the pumpkin coach around in a circle and out the gate.

Once on the road, things smoothed out a little as the two hamster-quail figured out how to work together.

"Verrrry good," said the fairy behind them, trilling the *R*s happily. "Verrrry good. Now let's all go to the ball togetherrrr!"

CHAPTER 21

By the time the pumpkin carriage reached the castle, Harriet was sweating under her feathers and Wilbur was panting.

"The interesting thing," she qwerked, "is that quail don't sweat. They cool off by panting. So we're still sort of *us* on the inside."

"And if you look at the carriage, it's got kind of pumpkin vine accents," continued Harriet. "And the newts and Stinky couldn't talk. So the fairy can't really change what we are, just the shape."

"Uh-huh," qwerked Wilbur. "Incidentally, I'm about to die."

"Stay with me, Wilbur. We're almost there. Now into the turn . . ."

The two quail turned into the stable yard. Ralph came out to meet them.

. . . HUH.

"Ralph!" qwerked Harriet. "Ralph, it's us!"

Well, that was what she meant to say.

She got as far as "Qwe—" when the door of the carriage slammed open and the fairy godmouse jumped out.

Harriet clamped her beak shut and gave Ralph what she hoped was a meaningful look.

"Ma'am," said Ralph politely to the fairy. "Are you here for the ball?"

"Oh, yes," said the fairy. She snapped her fingers.

Whiskerella slowly climbed down. Her lower lip trembled as if she might cry. But she took a deep breath and lifted her chin.

Attagirl! thought Harriet. *Keep the fairy happy until I get out of this harness! And then I'm gonna give her* such *a kicking!*

Ralph looked at her, shifted his feet, and said, "These are different quail, miss."

... YES. YES, THEY ARE. VERY DIFFERENT AND—AND *SPECIAL* QUAIL. PLEASE TAKE VERY GOOD CARE OF THEM.

WELL, THEY DON'T LOOK TO HAVE WOBBLY QUAIL LIKE THE OTHERS DID, SO THAT'S GOOD.

"Wobbly quail," muttered the fairy. "Good grief. You see what I'm saving you from? Marry a prince and you'll never have to think of quail again!"

". . . quail foot health is important," mumbled Ralph, but he said it under his breath and avoided the fairy's eyes.

"Thank you for your help," said Whiskerella, ignoring the fairy. "I took the others to the vet because you suggested it."

The tips of Ralph's ears turned bright red.

Whiskerella might have said more, but the fairy waved her wand and vanished abruptly.

"I'll be right here," her voice assured Whiskerella. "Now, let's go to the ball!"

Ralph gazed after them. "Fairies," he said. "Huh." And then, glumly, "Wobbly quail. Three times I've met her, and the only thing I've talked to her about is quail feet." He smacked himself in the forehead. "'You look lovely, miss.' 'It's a fine evening, miss.' 'This is an interesting carriage, miss, where was it made?' Ugh. No, I went straight to foot diseases. Get it together, Ralph!"

He took Harriet and Wilbur's reins and backed them toward the carriage-yard, still talking to himself. Up in the driver's seat, Misty looked excruciatingly uncomfortable.

Harriet had been planning on revealing her identity to Ralph immediately, but now it was going to be very awkward. She exchanged pained glances with Wilbur.

Oh, well . . . thought Harriet. "Ralph!" she qwerked. "It's us!"

Ralph petted Wilbur's beak morosely. He didn't appear to hear her.

Wilbur looked startled. Having one's beak petted is a surprising experience when one isn't used to owning a beak at all.

QWERK QWERK **QWERK!**

"Sorry," said Ralph.

"That's better—" Harriet started to say—and then Ralph started scratching her beak instead.

"Didn't mean to make you jealous," said Ralph.

Harriet thought about pecking him very hard.

"I don't think he can understand us," qwerked

Wilbur. "The fairy said nobody who wasn't a quail would understand us."

"But Ralph understands Quail! At least normally!"

"Right, well . . . I don't think the spell will let us explain ourselves. At least, not to Ralph."

Ralph unharnessed them and gathered up the reins. "You're still welcome to come inside," he said to Misty. "You don't have to stay on the carriage."

Misty slipped down from the seat, to Ralph's obvious surprise. She nodded at him.

"You're coming? Well—wonderful! Let me put these two fellows in the paddock and I'll show you where you can get a bite to eat."

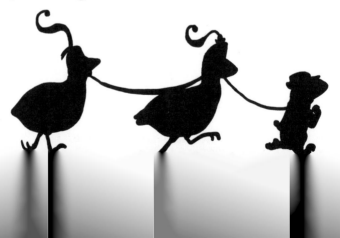

Ralph left them in the paddock and shut the gate. Other quail looked at them curiously.

Misty couldn't say anything. She came up between them and hugged both their necks fiercely.

"Don't worry," qwerked Harriet. "Don't—oh, I know you can't understand me! But we'll work something out! Nobody's getting forced into a happily ever after while I'm around to prevent it!"

Misty released them and followed after Ralph.

Ralph shoved his hands in his pockets as the two slouched away.

From inside the stable, Harriet heard a familiar qwerking. She spun around, stamping her scaly feet with excitement.

"Mumfrey!" she called. "Mumfrey, it's me! *Harriet!*"

CHAPTER 22

There was some thumping and rattling, and then Mumfrey emerged from the stable, looking confused. "Harriet?" he qwerked. *"Boss?"* He looked in both directions.

"Over here! The two white quail!"

Mumfrey stared at them, astonishment written across his beak.

"Yes! It's me! And this is Wilbur! You can understand me?"

Mumfrey looked pained.

"Never mind the accent!" qwerked Harriet. "I'm a quail!"

"I . . . I got that, Boss . . ." said Mumfrey.

There was a momentary pause while Harriet and Mumfrey and Wilbur all looked at one another.

"Are you going to ask why we're quail?" asked Wilbur.

"Because you finally realized that being a quail is awesome?" Mumfrey frowned. "But wait, who's going to bring me birdseed? We can't all be quail!"

Harriet stifled a sigh. Quail do not think quite like hamsters do. They aren't dumb, but it is perhaps most accurate to say that they are mostly intelligent about things that matter to quail.

"It's a fairy curse," said Wilbur. "And we can't seem to talk to people. Err . . . non-quail people."

"And we need to get into the castle to the ball!" said Harriet. "And stop that fairy!"

Most quail would have given up in bafflement at this point. But Mumfrey was an extraordinary bird, hardened by battle, and by years of living with Harriet. He nodded.

"There's a door in the garden," he qwerked. "It should be big enough . . ."

The garden door led to the scullery, which is the room where people do dishes. (Harriet had been bitterly disappointed to learn that it had nothing to do with skulls.) The dedicated dishwashers were known as "scullions," and one was staring at them right now.

"Bob!" he called over his shoulder. "Bob, there's a . . . a bunch of quail here . . . ?"

"Do they need washing?" shouted Bob.

"I don't know. Do we wash quail?"

Harriet had had enough. She stomped up to the

door, pushed the startled scullion aside, and tried to work the lower doorknob with her beak.

"Bob, it's trying to open the door!"

". . . gnrnrrggh . . ." Harriet muttered into the doorknob. It was like trying to grab a slippery ball with a pair of tongs. She felt an intense longing for her missing thumbs.

"I'll do it," qwerked Mumfrey. He leaned over and turned the doorknob neatly, then pulled the door open.

"Where did you learn to do that?" asked Harriet, amazed.

THEY KEEP THE REALLY *GOOD* BIRDSEED BEHIND A DOOR LIKE THIS IN THE STABLE.

"Bob, the door's open," reported the scullion.

"Well, close it, then!" shouted Bob.

"The quail are in the scullery, Bob!"

"Then get them out!"

"Errr . . . I don't think they want to leave, Bob . . ."

The scullery was full of dishes. Then it was full of quail. Then it was full of crashing noises and broken dishes. Harriet, Wilbur, and Mumfrey squeezed through the door, one after another, leaving a trail of smashed crockery in their wake.

CHAPTER 23

Harriet charged from the scullery, past the kitchen full of startled cooks, and into the castle proper. The kitchen led to a long hall, which led to the dining rooms and the ballroom.

"This way!" cried Harriet. "Quick!"

Wilbur and Mumfrey were right behind her, all of them running down the hallway.

A servant saw them coming, let out a squeal of terror, and dove out of the way.

As a quail, running on a rug was . . . complicated. The rug kept trying to slide out from under Harriet's enormous clawed feet.

She managed to skid around a decorative table with a couple of candlesticks on it. She was just congratulating herself on this when she heard a crash and a "Qwerrgghaaaaak!" and Wilbur wiped out on it.

Mumfrey was quite good at running as a quail, having had a lifetime of experience, and so dodged around Wilbur easily. Unfortunately, he yanked the rug sideways when he did, pulling it completely out from under Harriet.

Harriet found herself flying through the air, and remembered, belatedly, that she had wings.

I can fly?

Wait, I can *fly!*

Flapping madly, she turned her fall into a long, out-of-control glide. She decapitated a vase full of flowers and knocked a portrait of her great-great-great-grandmother off the wall, but she did not—quite—fall.

Like an enormous Ping-Pong ball, like a feathery blimp with no steering, she bounced off the walls, careened around a corner, and *there* was the entrance to the ballroom.

The herald who announced people's names stared at her with his mouth hanging open, but Harriet didn't care. She could announce herself perfectly well. She swept the herald out of the way and flung herself into the ballroom. There was a squawk behind her as Mumfrey ran over the herald.

"Stop the happily ever after!" shouted Harriet. Which naturally came out "QWERK!"

Princes and princesses, dukes and duchesses, marquis and viscounts and earls, all stared at her.

So did Ratpunzel, Harriet's parents, and Whiskerella.

The music faltered. The band stopped playing.

The couples stopped dancing. You could have heard a pin drop in the ballroom.

There was a second, muffled squawk as Wilbur, still wearing most of the end table, ran over the herald.

"Oh, I say!" said the bat ambassador, sounding delighted. "There's quail in the ballroom!"

"Was this part of the entertainment?" asked Harriet's mother weakly.

WELL, IT'S CERTAINLY ENTERTAINING, IS IT NOT?

YES, BUT THE DAMAGE TO THE FLOORS ... WHO LET THEM IN? AND IS THAT *MUMFREY?*

"If it's Mumfrey, Harriet's around here some-where," said the hamster king. He helped himself to another sandwich.

"That doesn't mean that there's going to be less damage!" said the queen.

"Oh, no," said her father. "Quite the opposite, I expect." He sounded resigned about it. "I told you we should just name her Collateral Damage, but you said Harriet was a much better name for a girl."

The bat ambassador put a claw over his mouth to keep from laughing.

Harriet looked around wildly. There was no point in trying to talk, was there? Everybody was just going to see a quail, and the spell would keep her from qwerking an explanation to those people who actually understood quail-qwerks.

She ground her beak in frustration. So much for subtlety. It was trampling time.

It is rather difficult to trample people without hurting them, but feathers helped. Harriet began shoving princes aside with her wings. "Get to Whiskerella!" she qwerked. "And find that fairy!"

"On it, Boss!" qwerked Mumfrey.

"I can't get this table off my head!" qwerked Wilbur.

"Mad quail!" screamed someone. (Harriet suspected that it was Prince C.)

"Do something!" yelled the hamster queen.

The hamster king gazed mournfully at his sandwich. "Be a dear," he called to the herald, "and go get someone from the stables to wrangle these quail, will you?"

Harriet saw Whiskerella and began shoving through the crowd. Hamsters bounced off her feathery chest.

Whiskerella looked terrified. Harriet could tell that she didn't know whether to run toward Harriet (in hopes of being saved) or away (in case the fairy did something awful to Harriet).

"Qwergghkk!" *Splat.* Wilbur, unable to see his feet over the table around his neck, fell over the

sandwich table. There was
a brief, localized rain of
cucumber slices.

Harriet was nearly to Whiskerella. She still
couldn't see the fairy.

She was stretching out her wings to put protec-
tively around the beautiful hamster when someone stepped forward.

"Begone, feathered fiend!" he shouted.

It was Prince A, and he was holding a sword.

CHAPTER 24

Halt!" cried Prince A.

"I've already halted," said Harriet, annoyed. "You can't yell *Halt!* when somebody's already stopped."

But of course, all the prince heard was "qwerk-qwerk-qwerkggha-werk."

"Get behind me!" said the prince to Whiskerella. "I'll protect you!"

"Protect me from what?"

THE
MAD QUAIL,
OF COURSE!

Whiskerella looked at him like he was an idiot. So did Harriet.

"I don't think she's mad," said Whiskerella. (This was wrong. Harriet was, in fact, furious.)

"You can't be too careful!" said Prince A. "It may have rabies!"

"Quail don't get rabies!" yelled Harriet, which came out "QWERRRKK!"

"There, you see? Clearly rabid! It'll be foaming at the beak shortly!"

Harriet really wanted to launch into a diatribe about how birds really can't get rabies and wouldn't foam at the beak and furthermore how Prince A was an idiot who had probably never ridden a quail in his life, but since all he would hear would be "qwerk," she didn't. There is nothing more infuriating than delivering a really good diatribe to someone who isn't listening.

Also, at that moment she heard a familiar voice behind her say, "Oh dear!"

It was Ralph.

"Ralph!" shouted the hamster king. "Good man! Why are these quail in here?"

"I don't know, Your Majesticness," said Ralph.

"I'm sorry! They're not our quail—well, that's Mumfrey, obviously, but the white quail are from somewhere else."

"Mumfrey, have I led you astray?" asked Harriet.

"Constantly, Boss," said Mumfrey. "It's basically what you do."

"Well, so long as we're clear . . ."

"Frankly," said the hamster queen, "it's a lot more likely that Harriet led them all astray! Where is she? You can't tell me she's not behind this!"

"Errr . . . she's in the bathroom," said Ratpunzel helpfully.

SHE'S BEEN IN THE BATHROOM AN AWFULLY LONG TIME . . .

"Well, these things happen," said the king. "I once spent an entire October in the bathroom. It was very restful."

The queen stared at her husband for a moment, then turned to Ralph. "Get these quail out of here! The floors—the ambassador's ball—"

"Oh, don't worry about me," said the ambassador. "I haven't had this much fun since the Duchess of Umberwall went sleepwalking in the middle of a battlefield and beat the enemy champion in her nightgown."

Harriet made a mental note to get to know the Duchess of Umberwall immediately.

At that point, three things happened more or less simultaneously.

Prince A, apparently thinking that Harriet was a dangerous animal that might attack at any time, lunged forward with his sword—

—the fairy re-appeared—

—and a viscountess shouted, at the top of her

lungs, "Someone has *widdled* in the *punch bowl!*" and fell over in a dead faint.

CHAPTER 25

Prince Archibald's sword work was as dreadful as the rest of him. He missed Harriet by a mile. Harriet wondered how she was supposed to disarm somebody when she didn't have hands— did she stand on one leg? Use her beak? There was something weird about grabbing somebody's sword with your face.

Fortunately, at that point Mumfrey simply bit his wrist to make him drop his sword.

"That's right, I will!" qwerked Harriet. "You can't *force* people to be happy!"

"I don't want your happily ever after!" said Whiskerella. "I just want you to leave me alone! I'm tired of balls! I'm tired of princes!"

Prince A, still clutching his wrist where Mumfrey had nipped him, looked up. "What? How dare you!?"

Stinky, recognizing a familiar voice, came out from behind the punchbowl and galloped across the dance floor toward Whiskerella, leaving small, excited puddles in his wake.

"Now, Mumfrey . . ." said Ralph in coaxing tones. "I know there's a lot going on and you're upset, but let's all go back to the stable and get some nice birdseed . . ."

"Qwerk!" said Mumfrey, which was Quail for "I *would* like some birdseed but I am rather busy right now, and also have you noticed that this quail is actually Harriet?"

"Huh?" said Ralph. "The what?"

"Tell him I'm under a spell!" qwerked Harriet.

"She's under a spell," qwerked Mumfrey.

"She is?"

"Ralph," said the hamster king, "I appreciate that you're trying to have a chat with Mumfrey, but

could you get the quail out of the ballroom first?
Or at least get the one out of the sandwiches?"

"Tell him the one in the sandwiches is Wilbur,"
ordered Harriet.

Mumfrey dutifully relayed this information.
"Qwerk qwerk qwerka-qwerk . . ."

"Happiness can't be forced!" yelled Whiskerella.

"The heck it can't!" the fairy yelled back.

"Sir," said Ralph. "I mean sire. I mean Your Kingness. Uh—Mumfrey says that these quail are actually Harriet and Wilbur."

Harriet nodded vigorously.

Her father looked at her. He looked at Ralph. He looked back at her.

"Well," he said. "All right, then."

I HOPE YOU KNOW WE'LL LOVE YOU WHETHER YOU'RE A QUAIL OR A HAMSTER OR . . . WHATEVER. YOU'RE STILL OUR LITTLE GIRL.

Harriet put her wing over her face. She appre-

ciated that her father was trying to be support-
ive, but a little less support and a little more fairy
curse breaking would have been nice.

Ralph yelled, "Look out, Ha—Princess!"

Harriet yanked her wing away from her eyes and saw Prince B and Prince C approaching, from opposite sides, waving swords of their own. Possibly they hadn't understood that she was a princess, or possibly they didn't care.

Backward was Mumfrey. Forward was Whiskerella. That only left one direction.

She launched herself into the air, flapping madly, and at that moment, the clock struck midnight.

BONG! BONG! BONG! BONG! BONG! BONG! BONG! BONG! BONG! BONG! BONG! BONG! BONG! BONG! BONG!

CHAPTER 26

Harriet waited to change back . . . and didn't.

"Not this time!" screamed the fairy. "Everyone stays the way they are until Whiskerella is swept off her feet!"

Some birds, such as hummingbirds, hover like helicopters. And some birds, such as quail, hover like bowling balls. Harriet plummeted to the ground.

Fortunately, her fall was broken by Princes B and C. All three went down in a heap. Harriet tried to roll, knocked into Whiskerella, and she went down too. A pair of dancers who had, some-how, still been trying to waltz fell over the fairy.

"Midnight!" cried the bat ambassador. "The ball has ended! It is time for the unmasking!"

"Yes!" said the fairy, sounding a bit muffled. "Yes, it's time to unmask!"

Normally the unmasking was greeted with cheers or sounds of anticipation. This time, it was met with groans.

The ballroom looked like a battlefield. Most of the guests had fled or wedged themselves in the corners of the room. Ratpunzel and the rat prince had taken shelter behind an overturned table. Ralph and Mumfrey stood in the middle of the room, looking very out of place. Wilbur was trying to get a tablecloth off his head. The hamster king was looking for undamaged sandwiches. The hamster queen had her eyes closed and her hands over her mouth.

Harriet sat up groggily. Her beak was clogged with fairy dust. There was something on the ground in front of her.

It was a glass slipper.

It occurred to her that she was probably sitting on Whiskerella. She got to her feet and began trying to drag the other hamster loose from the princes.

Whiskerella's mask had come off. Her other shoe was lost somewhere under Prince C's backside. She was no longer the most beautiful hamster in the world. She looked as tired as Harriet felt.

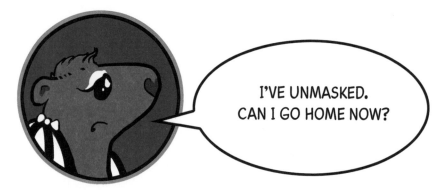

I'VE UNMASKED.
CAN I GO HOME NOW?

"NO!" screamed the fairy, crawling out from under the dancers.

She had seen better days. Her wings were crumpled and her wand was bent. The twinkle in her eyes had become a furious blaze.

"Princes!" she shouted, stabbing her wand toward Whiskerella. "She's unmasked! Look!"

The princes looked.

THE BEAUTIFUL STRANGER, YOU NUMBSKULLS!

The princes looked at Whiskerella.

"Don't be stupid," said Prince A. "That's not her. She's not nearly beautiful enough. The other hamster was much prettier."

Despite having said something similar a few days earlier, Harriet had a strong urge to peck Prince Archibald right in his smug little nose. How dare anybody insult Whiskerella like that! Whiskerella was worth a dozen princes! Maybe two dozen!

Fortunately, someone else stepped in for her.

"Excuse me, Your Prince-ness—"

"Oh, bravo!" Without taking his eyes off the scene, the bat ambassador stretched out a wing and snagged another canapé.

"Ralph," said the hamster king mildly, "we do not solve our problems with violence."

"Sorry, sir."

"We certainly do not solve them by punching princes."

"Yes, sir . . ." Ralph hung his head.

"As punishment, I am afraid I will be forced to give you a raise and a promotion," said the hamster king. "You are now the Royal Head Groom. I trust that will make you think about what you've done."

Ralph blinked.

"No!" shouted the fairy, stamping her foot. "Stop! We're not done here!"

Prince B and Prince C looked panicked. "Who, us?"

"The glass slipper!" yelled the fairy. "Pick it up!"

"Um. Ew," said Prince B. "It's all sweaty. It's gonna smell like feet."

Prince C looked like he was about to say something more, and then he saw the expression on the fairy's face and hurriedly picked up the shoe.

"Now, put it on!"

I . . .
I DON'T
THINK
IT'LL FIT
ME . . .

"Not you! Put it on *her!*" The fairy was so furious now that little flecks of spit were raining down whenever she spoke. "The slipper belongs to the beautiful stranger! If you put it on her, you'll see that she's the one you've been dancing with!"

Prince C looked at the glass slipper in his hand as if it were poisonous and might attack at any time.

Harriet pushed Whiskerella behind her. "Qwerk!" she yelled, which was Quail for "Just try it!"

"You!" screamed the fairy. "You've ruined everything! They were supposed to take the slipper and go through the kingdom looking for the girl whose foot fit into it, and then she would have been beautiful forever and had a happily ever after, but *you* had to get involved!"

Harriet stared at her. So did everyone else.

"I—why—you—" The fairy spluttered in rage. "Shut up! It's a great plan! It would have worked if everyone hadn't stuck their noses in! Well, now you'll pay the price!"

SPLUTTER
SIZZLE
CRACKLE

The broken wand made a noise. It was not a magical noise. It sounded more like broken machinery.

"What?" The fairy slapped her palm against the star a few times. "Why won't this thing work right?"

The star fell off and hit the ground with a *ker-CLUNK!*

"Fine! Good enough!" The fairy flung the wand aside, snatched the slipper from Prince C, and advanced on Whiskerella. "I'll do it myself!"

Whiskerella put up her arm to ward off the terrible slipper. The fairy lunged forward . . .

. . . directly into a puddle of widdle.

CHAPTER 27

The fairy's foot skidded out from under her. She flung her arms up, trying to catch herself. The glass slipper went flying across the ballroom (the bat ambassador ducked) and smashed into a wall, where it shattered into dust.

The fairy herself plowed into Whiskerella, who jumped out of the way, skidded to avoid *another* puddle—Stinky had been *very* nervous—tripped on a fallen sandwich, and went sprawling.

Ralph caught her before she hit the floor.

"Ralph?" said Whiskerella weakly. "You caught me?"

"Uh," said Ralph. "Yes. Sorry, miss. I didn't mean—I mean, I meant to, but—um—"

"It's all right," said Whiskerella leaning against him. "It's fine."

Ralph began to blush. The tips of his ears turned bright red. But he didn't put Whiskerella down, either.

The fairy stood up. She looked around for her wand, for the slipper, for anything, and saw the two hamsters embracing.

NO . . .

"I believe," said the bat ambassador, "that the night's entertainment has run its course, madam."

The fairy glared at him. "The spell isn't done!"

"Oh, I don't know. The mysterious stranger has

been swept off her feet, has she not?" He waved a
wing at Whiskerella and Ralph.

"Fine . . ." The bat ambassador rolled his eyes.
"Young man! Ralph!"

"Y-yes, Your Ambassador-ness?" asked Ralph, looking up guiltily. He had been gazing into Whiskerella's eyes.

"By the power vested in me as an official of the kingdom of bats, I pronounce you ruler of the Second Crag of Extreme Lower Batavia. You are now a prince."

BUT—UH—

Whiskerella put her finger over his lips. Ralph blinked.

Harriet started to qwerk something, but suddenly her feathers shrank and turned to fur.

Her neck retracted on itself like a tape measure rolling up—*sssnnnnrrrp!* Her tail dwindled away to a nub and her beak softened and turned into lips.

All of this was, if not painful, at least very weird and uncomfortable, but fortunately it was over quickly.

"Oh, hello dear," said the hamster king. "If we're all done here, could the guards please come take this fairy away?"

The fairy sniffed. "I'll see myself out," she said, and walked to the door with as much dignity as someone squishing quietly from lizard widdle could.

"But sir!" whispered Ralph as soon as the fairy was out of earshot. "I don't want to be a prince! I'm not good at princing!"

"Don't worry about it," said the bat ambassador. "The Second Crag of Lower Batavia is about three feet tall and six inches wide. It's in my guest bedroom. Your princeness is purely symbolic."

One by one, the guests filed out of the ballroom. Wilbur took Mumfrey back to the stables. Misty came in and collected Stinky from a corner. The hamster queen, looking around the room, declared "I am going to bed" in much the same tones that one would declare war on a rival nation.

Ralph and Whiskerella looked at each other. They looked away.

"Um," said Ralph. "I . . . uh." His ears were turning pink again.

Whiskerella tucked her arm through his and led him toward the door. "I want you to tell me everything you know about quail diseases," she said firmly.

"R . . . really?" stammered Ralph. "Well—uh—there's bent gizzard and wogglebeak and . . ."

Then it was only the king, and the ambassador, and Harriet.

"You found a way around it," said Harriet. Her body still felt unpleasantly tingly, as if parts of it had been asleep. "I was afraid Dad was going to have to adopt him."

The bat ambassador grinned down at her. "It is what ambassadors do," he said. "We can't all hit people with swords until they get along, you know."

"It's worked so far," muttered Harriet.

"The *Pax Hamstera* . . . ha!" He ruffled her hair with a claw. "You must come to the bat kingdom someday, young Harriet. You would find it most interesting. And now—it has been a very long night, and I think perhaps I shall seek my bed before dawn for once."

And then it was only Harriet and her father.

The king sighed. "Still, it makes your mother happy. And I guess it worked out."

"More or less," said Harriet. "More or less. And we averted a happily ever after, anyway."

"I want you to know that I don't love you any more as a hamster than a quail," said the hamster king. "Or any less. I mean, whichever you want to be."

"It's okay, Dad," said Harriet. She patted him on the arm. "Err . . . thank you?"

"You should have some of these sandwiches," said the king. "They're only a little squashed."

Harriet took a sandwich. The bread was a little squishy, but the cucumber was as crisp as ever.

"I also don't care if you ever get married," said the king. "To a prince or anybody else. You'll still be my favorite daughter."

"I'm your *only* daughter," said Harriet.

"So you *know* I'm telling the truth."

They sat in the ruined ballroom together, munching companionably, while the sun rose once more over the hamster kingdom, and, somewhere, another adventure.

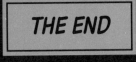

THE END

DON'T MISS THESE OTHE[R]

URSULA

MOKING HOT BOOKS FROM VERNON!

DRAGONBREATH
NO SUCH THING AS GHOSTS
URSULA VERNON

DRAGONBREATH
REVENGE OF THE HORNED BUNNIES
URSULA VERNON

DRAGONBREATH
WHEN FAIRIES GO BAD
URSULA VERNON

DRAGONBREATH
NIGHTMARE OF THE IGUANA
URSULA VERNON

HAMSTER PRINCESS
HARRIET the INVINCIBLE
Ursula Vernon

HAMSTER PRINCESS
OF MICE and MAGIC
Ursula Vernon

HAMSTER PRINCESS
RATPUNZEL
Ursula Vernon

HAMSTER PRINCESS
GIANT TROUBLE
Ursula Vernon

HARRIET HAMSTEI

★ "MOVE OVER, BABYMOUSE, THERE'S A NEW RODENT IN TOWN!"
—*SCHOOL LIBRARY JOURNAL*, STARRED REVIEW

★ "HARRIET IS HER OWN HAMSTER, BUT SHE TAKES HER PLACE PROUDLY ALONGSIDE BOTH DANNY DRAGONBREATH AND BABYMOUSE. CREATIVELY FRESH AND FEMINIST, WITH LAUGHS ON EVERY SINGLE PAGE."
—*KIRKUS REVIEWS*, STARRED REVIEW

★ "A BOOK WITH ALL THE MAKINGS OF A HIT. READERS WILL BE LAUGHING THEMSELVES SILLY."
—*PUBLISHERS WEEKLY*, STARRED REVIEW

★ "A JOY TO READ, AND WE CAN ONLY HOPE THAT HARRIET—LONG MAY SHE REIGN—WILL RETURN IN LATER INSTALLMENTS."
—*BOOKLIST*, STARRED REVIEW

BONE IS A STAR!

★ "MAINTAINING A KEEN BALANCE BETWEEN SILLY AND SLY, THIS SEQUEL WILL HAVE READERS SNICKERING."
— *KIRKUS REVIEWS,* STARRED REVIEW

★ "AS HILARIOUS AS IT IS FUN. MAKE ROOM ON THE SHELVES FOR THIS NOT SO FRILLY PRINCESS."
— *SCHOOL LIBRARY JOURNAL,* STARRED REVIEW

"HARRIET IS AS DELIGHTFUL AS EVER. . . . AS LONG AS VERNON KEEPS HARRIET'S ADVENTURES COMING, FANS NEW AND OLD ARE BOUND TO KEEP READING THEM." — *BOOKLIST*

"THIS IS VINTAGE VERNON. CLEVER WORDPLAY, WONDERFUL CHARACTER BANTER, AND STINKY HUMOR MAKE THIS OUTING ANOTHER GIANT SUCCESS." — *KIRKUS REVIEWS*

ABOUT the AUTHOR

Ursula Vernon (www.ursulavernon.com) is an award-winning author and illustrator whose work has won a Hugo Award and a Nebula Award, and been nominated for the World Fantasy Award and an Eisner. She loves birding, gardening, and spunky heroines. She is the first to admit that she would make a terrible princess.